Hey,

Lost Child.

Hogoe Elimiera

Hey, Lost child by Hogoe Elimiera

Acknowledgments

For all those seeking guidance in a world of mazes,
and dead ends.

Table of content

I may never find someone
To convince me to make
a proper table of content
but once more what's the
fun in knowing where you
left off. Sometimes you need
to reread something, you
read before, for better
understanding.

I may also just be lazy.
Both ring valid.

Hey, Lost child by Hogoe Elimiera

You're not alone, you are lonely. I hope these words hug you tighter than a lover, suffocating the sadness within you and make way for growth and advancement.

Hey, Lost child by Hogoe Elimiera

Hey, Lost child by Hogoe Elimiera

Your being was so delicately created.
So pure in creation. So fragile in conception, so
worthy in existence. Your search towards answers,
how tired you must be, in a world where the road you
took that led to a maze of confusion may also be the
one that gives your purpose to your relevance.

Hey, Lost child by Hogoe Elimiera

Tears don't melt into your skin without leaving some
evidence. Eyes call for help, as they shade
themselves in red because your lips of hidden pink
are too silent to. Everything around you is calling for
the help you need because you have yet to. You've
hidden yourself, but your emotions reveal you.

Hey, Lost child by Hogoe Elimiera

Is it guidance you seek, or to be left alone.
Are you confused, or have you stopped looking.
Funny isn't it? To find guidance you must search for
it. To find a solution you must navigate through the
maze of illusion.

Did you ask yourself if you were happy? Or did you
just assume you were sad. Doesn't it make you a bit
mad, when you aren't sure which one you are. If you
want to live or crash into a moving car. Triggering
isn't it? The thoughts, yet familiar isn't it? The
Emotions.

Hey, Lost child by Hogoe Elimiera

Logic says you are worth a million. Yet the hourly wage says you're barely worth ten. You think you aren't worth anything, but you're wrong in the end. If you weren't ever of value your existence wouldn't have ever began.

Someone smiled at you this morning, but you didn't see, with you head faced to the ground. Your eyes open, yet your surrounding blurred. You didn't see the young child as they told their mother how amazing you looked. You didn't see the thoughts within that person's head as they admired your presence. You were too consumed into your sadness to notice the difference. Yet how could you, notice when your head is always faced in the same direction.

Hey, Lost child by Hogoe Elimiera

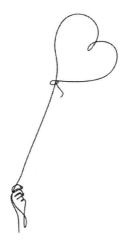

Lights on, yet the darkness still sinks into your presence. We were told darkness had not relevance where light resided. But maybe it wasn't directed towards the mind. In the mind: They coexist there, they befriend one another there. Yet as small as the darkness is, it tends to be the loudest. So, it made you blind to light and deaf to happiness.

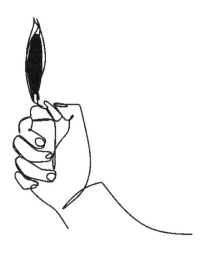

Were you in love or were you just the one loving.
Was it a heartbreak, or did you lose where you placed
it. What is lost can be found. What is broken can be
replaced, but you waste more money buying and
replacing, then putting it back where it was lost, and
once shattered.

Are they still saying it or are you replaying it. The echo of negativity you hear. Lost within your mind, found in the night, and present in the day. Did they say it, or did you think it for them. In the end the real question is why have you began to agree with them?

Hey, Lost child by Hogoe Elimiera

You live with yourself the longest, but you have begun to love yourself the least. Why is that so? Why are you weeping for the pain of another, and not yourself. Your tears are for the pain, but for the one feeling it you keep blaming them. Why are you dismissing yourself.

The wind around you longs to hug you. Steps you take chant in gratitude. The birds that soar long to fly beside you. The smile you gave saved a soul tonight. The door you held helped someone today. The thanks you said warmed a heart yesterday. Yet you never notice because you think you're nothing more than nothing more.

Hey, Lost child by Hogoe Elimiera

Are you worthless or have you just forgotten your self-worth. Are you hated by everyone you meet or have you more hate for yourself, so you've convinced yourself you aren't fun to be around. Are you unattractive or have you convinced yourself that your uniqueness is negative while comparing it to a circle of those that look alike.

A shark cannot live as a lion, within a jungle and rule as it does in the sea. As great it's abilities, as fearless as its dedication. A shark is nothing more than meat outside the sea, though a powerful force within the waves. Your abilities are there, sometimes your setting just doesn't allow you to identify it.

I once was sinking in a lake, fearfully I fought for my life. A hypocrite I was. I said at the age of thirteen: " I live to end my life but fight to save it when it is everything but me trying to take it away." How sad I wouldn't been to not have lived to see who I became today.

There's a higher self within you, that you have yet to discover. Rest within it, wrap it's arms around you as you would as a savior. Let it comfort the child within that is hurting for truth. Let it feed your attention. Let it be as it should be, for today you grow closer to know who you are to be, even if you were more confused that yesterday.

I am amazed by you, even though you don't know me.
I don't know what you're called but you amaze me.
You won't believe me but it's true. Even so you don't
know everyone that knows you outside your title. To
that someone you were the amazing person that
mended their sadness. To me you're the fighter that
keeps on trying.

Are you lost or have you just been following the wrong leader. Are you worthless or have you just been making the wrong people worthy of your kindness.

" I deserve to die" I once said. The old woman beside
me on the bench responded: " One day my child
everyone will be dead, but why live to end yourself
because of a current something when you aren't sure
of the wonderful everything that is coming ahead.
Bring it to an end now, you won't enjoy the start of
when your story truly begins, now that will be
something that hurts far worse than death.

Silence is soothing, tranquility is a muse, to watch as everything passes, to hear your heart pound in the silence, to be alone outside of loneliness. To be whole within the emptiness, that's the level of self-acceptance you should strive to be.

Like a sinking ship, sometimes one can over consume
what was to be relied on to keep afloat, so much so
that independence becomes lost to what was only to
be the assistance.

Sometimes, those that look down on others feel too small to admit they are actually looking up. Say you're welcome to their silent "thank you" Even if you don't hear it, just know sometimes, someone that " hates " it's not hate, but frustration that they aren't yet like you.

Hey, Lost child by Hogoe Elimiera

Hey, Lost child by Hogoe Elimiera

You easily say I love you, but you say it more than
you hear it said to you. Everyone else is saying it
enough, you just have been short on how often you
say it to yourself.

Hey, Lost child by Hogoe Elimiera

Why is it so hard to admit, that you have it. That
ability, that talent, that thing that makes you, you.
Have you dismissed it's value, finding it but
overlooking it's worth. Or are you hiding it's price
tag to make everyone else feel better.

You want to be loved but keep finding what you
thought was love to be a mistake, as it transforms into
what it really was: A contract of hidden intention.
Makes sense as to why it happened, you never loved
yourself to know what love was, so you allowed
everyone one else to write the conditions on what you
should do for them. Thinking you were doing it for
you.

Hey, Lost child by Hogoe Elimiera

If I were you, I would love you. If I were you, I would spoil you. If I were you, I would care for you. But I am not you. There are so many amazing things I would do for you, why miss them as you wait for someone else to do for you, what you should already be doing for yourself.

One day you smiled, in the presence of yourself, you laughed, at how funny you were. You raced to your room and was at peace with being alone. In the mirror you were the celebrity everyone wanted to be. You explored the abilities of the world. You allowed yourself to make mistakes and smiled at strangers, because your head was always held up high. Then you grew up, rather, did you really grow? Had the kid within you held more fearlessness than the person you've become?

If they never said sorry, I say it on their behalf. Some
people will never admit their fault. Some people
never have. Why do you imprison yourself for a
crime done against you, waiting for an apology to set
you free. You have the key, but it is up to you, who
you lock within the gates. Don't waste your life away,
locked in chains waiting for an " I am sorry." From
someone that " may" say it, even if you deserve it. In
the end I'll say again, for what they did: " I'm sorry."
I hope that played a role in your release.

No one else will create for you what you should do
for yourself. Everyone is far too busy trying to figure
out what they should do for themselves. Is it wrong?
In the end you don't feel whole because you've given
too much of yourself away, thinking you were going
to receive pieces of everyone else, to fill the gaps that
have been created. Everyone isn't you, so stop
treating everyone with the sacrifice you think you
should be receiving.

trafalgarssquare

Have you thanked yourself yet? For being alive.
Even if you want to die, have you thanked yourself
yet? Something within you believes in you enough to
keep you going, even when you feel like you aren't
moving.

When you find a lover, I hope it is after you learned to love yourself. I hope it's after you planted a garden of seeds that have overpowered the weeds, but act like weeds themselves. You keep coming back, with more love for yourself after a hit, you resurrect without limit. I hope when you find a lover, it is after you learned to love yourself. I hope so. So that you may know if you are being cheated or treated pricelessly as you are worth.

You are majestic, you are purposefully. You are everything you should be, you just have yet to discover who you will be. That person, that person you will meet, after your transformation, is and always will be thankful for who you are now. A winner isn't a winner without facing some trials.

Most of the time what a person can say and what a
person shouldn't say don't always align you can
correct a person for wrongfully doing so but you
can't harass a person into an apology, then in the end
your energy is wasted and your efforts out of
hypocrisy, for wanting to hear an apology for
something you never intend to forgive.

One night you will give a genuine smile to yourself
like you once did as you gave fake ones to appear
okay. One evening in the silence of your room you
will feel at ease and protected with the presence of
yourself as you once did when you convinced
yourself you were at peace though you felt lonely in
a crowed room. One night you will, rather than fake
the day with smiles and mourn in the night. Your
day's joy will be as genuine as the evening's
happiness.

Hey, Lost child by Hogoe Elimiera

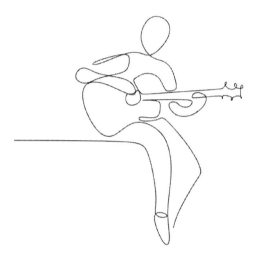

Is it truthfully not worth it or did you dismiss it
because you haven't given your work time to flourish.
Like a bird that walks on the ground, because it's too
scared to fly. You've limited your abilities because
you won't even try.

Hey, Lost child by Hogoe Elimiera

Will you never make it, or have you become your own critic, replaying your own dismiss as if a song, left to hear tomorrow. Rewinding all the lyrics that make you sad, in the end you were never awful at what you did, you weren't even bad. You just never gave yourself the chance to fall in love with it long enough to defend it.

Did you hear that? The whisper of solitude that
kissed your neck? Did you see that? The wave of
tomorrow that caressed your cheek. Your eyes have
gone blind to your wonders, your senses have died to
the beauty. You have cheated yourself, but you are
also the one that can reclaim and title yourself worthy.

You can breathe underwater, and eventually learn how to avoid drowning; you just have to figure out how to breathe well enough on land, and master walking without falling.

To better understand yourself you must also understand your surroundings. You can't survive in an ocean, if you aren't aware of the possibilities of the sea, or the dangers of its waves.

Hey, Lost child by Hogoe Elimiera

Who are you surrounded by, who do they make themselves out to be? Are they truly your friends or are you too lonely to label anyone your enemy, in fear of having to be your own priority.

I value you

1-4

1.

I don't love you. I value you. I take emotion to the
actions you display. I feel at peace when your
presence reveals itself. I grow accustomed to your
love and its relevance.

2.

I don't love you. I value you. In valuing you my mind
is at rest while my heart never sleeps. No empty
words are said from me to you. Because in this most
authentic state. It's not enough to just love you.

3

I value you and all that you make yourself
out to be. The way you embrace my being.
The way you allow me to be aware of the
humanity beneath this shell compartment
I've carved into myself.

4

I could never simply love you
I value you.
In valuing you, I love you
I love you beyond, measures that loving you
alone could ever do.
Surpass the limit that love gives
waiting just beneath the horizon there awaits:

" I value you. "

Whether yourself, family, friend, or a lover, life requires being and Identity. Being is the state of physical awareness. More often than not, one gives no credit of value towards themselves, or those around them. To better understand the people around you, you have to first figure out the value of those people. In a body of water, that you rush to fight against you are sure to drown. I love you is easily spoken but the meaning differs among who it is being said to.

A commonality that lingers along with I love you is the format of appreciation. To tell someone you love them is to bring to awareness the value you hold to them. To value someone really navigates the direction to which you treat them, being yourself, your family, friend or a lover. To value someone is to let go of possible fear. Once that fear is diluted it becomes much easier to try and understand how to better maintain the situation you are residing in.

Help, but don't be a servant

1-4

Hey, Lost child by Hogoe Elimiera

1.

Are we to each other as ocean and moon, or ocean
and plastic. Do we bring value to one another's
motions or is the other feeding off of the home one
provides and killing the lively hood that is trying to
flourish.

2.

As great the distance between land and space, I'd
rather be as the craters of the moon above
contributing to the dancing of the tides, as it hugs the
sand, before it subsides lingering along with it, it's
foam.

3.

The gravity that hugs us apart but intertwines us as
one. I rather that be the distance's source, than to be
like plastic or an unknown residing beneath your
waves. If my home is within you, I suffocate, feeling
out of place, and slowing dim your light along with it.

4.

Selfishly If I become the one with harm to you, I will also whine up harming myself, yet only to stay because of the comfort you give, and dependency on your benefits, rather than to compliment you as I do, being your moon. To do as I can to make you feel alive, but still be independent in my own sky, at the same time.

Hey, Lost child by Hogoe Elimiera

Hey, Lost child by Hogoe Elimiera

Whether it's you, or everyone else around you, one has to understand their role. The relationship the moon has with the ocean is a beautiful one. One resides in assistance with the other, but have their own title of relevance without it, yet still can't be complete without the other.

You aren't meant to be lost in yourself, you are meant to be aware of who it is you are to be, in order to work towards that. You aren't meant to be lost in family, friends, or your partner. You are meant to assist them where they lack, as they do the same for you. The moon gives the ocean its tides as a form of strength and balance and the ocean gives the moon a planet to call its own.

There is calmness and serenity in the ocean, but there's fear in the sinking. You realize, it's a dream and not a nightmare, the moment you learn to stop fighting against yourself, and start to listen to the language of the waves around you.

Hey, Lost child by Hogoe Elimiera

Hey, Lost child by Hogoe Elimiera

Using words as a life jacket.
Swimming within emotions.
Discovering life after death
of who you use to be.
Becoming aware of who
you want to be and those
around you that can take
You there.

To the stranger whose name you know, I hope they keep surprising you. I hope they keep alarming you. I hope they keep surpassing your expectations. To the stranger you know so well I hope they keep accomplishing everything you thought they wouldn't. To the stranger living within you, I hope one day you come to acknowledge the stranger that keeps loving you. I hope you meet them sometime soon and say hello. I hope you eventually meet the real you.

I wish you a future with no past. Weird isn't it? No past? Let's say it this way: I hope you take into the future your present self, alone. Acknowledge the past you that brought you here but allow that person to stay where they learned their lesson, and take with you the one you've become.

A which point do you remind yourself who you truly are. At which point do you start valuing your time. At which point do you start embracing your existence. The longer it takes for the union to take place, the longer you give yourself away for less than you ever amounted to, even at your lowest.

Dear lost child,

I am not more aware than you, I have just managed to
understand the steps. I haven't even started yet. Well
I have, but often I don't finish. Yet, there's beauty in
the journey. The awareness of the process. The trials
of endurance, that's where I've come to reside. No
better than the one searching, but far more found than
I am lost. I wish better for you.

Your experiences have tongue-tied themselves into silence. Too shy to admit pain, too coy to say otherwise. Though your words don't say it your spirit shows it. You have yet to address it. I hope you do so soon. Pressing silent on pain only overplays its tune.

Who wrote the book of love. I hope you meet them
soon. Hidden in it's silent abilities I hope you
discover them too. I hope you figure it out before
they do. The one that wrote the book that is, so you
know if everything they are saying is actually true, or
you might believe them simply because they said I
love you.

It's good to be good. It's kind to be welcoming.
Don't be so good that you welcome those that aren't
good to you, assuming that they will change into
someone new. You have yet to figure out who to
avoid giving your attention to, they too have yet to
figure out who they should value.

Hey, Lost child by Hogoe Elimiera

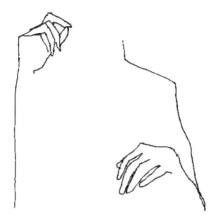

You make mistakes because mistakes make you who you are to be, if you made none, thus far, you aren't anywhere near who you will be.

Hey, Lost child by Hogoe Elimiera

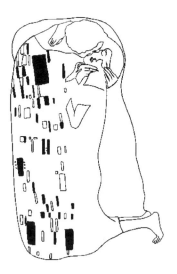

validation is not wrong, nor is it wrong to consider the acknowledgment of another but it is dangerous to get wrapped up in the opinion of someone to be your source of motivation.

Excellence and perfection aren't the same thing.
They speak different dialects of the same nation. Like
a stair and an elevator, they both go through motion.
But like glass and metal, both similar to creating
something new: yet, one shatters rather easily despite
its appearance of assumed clarity.

At times bruises are made to remind blood how protecting the skin is. Tears clog up one's throat to remind the lungs how sweet air tastes. Legs fail to walk, and hit the ground to remind the body, how high it has risen. Pain is meant to remind the heart how soothing happiness is.

Hey, Lost child by Hogoe Elimiera

See your own beauty

1-4

1.

The same sun that sets for me, may not have the same
color of pastel orange as it does when it sets for you.
It may be a masterpiece illustrated in deep sea purple,
but mine will forever be the most beautiful to me,
because it's the one I see.

2.

When I look down, or return to showcase the
wonders I saw outside the sunlight ray might've
changed its mind. Becoming a blue or lavender. The
way I caresses my fingers when I begin to worry, to
the way my skin reacts to a sudden laugh.

3.

Our likeness exceeds our differences, but our
likenesses aren't identical in admiration. We may
resort to familiarity in interests, but we'd never
become the same person.

4.

You should never be so lost that you try to clone your self into a copy of someone else. Missing all the experiences and wonders you were meant to see for yourself.

Hey, Lost child by Hogoe Elimiera

You're not yet familiar with all your problems, you have to know what you need to fix before you can ask for the guidance to fix it. Too many people give opinions, otherwise. Leaving you tangled before you even figure out what you needed to ask. This only sets yourself back.

Hey, Lost child by Hogoe Elimiera

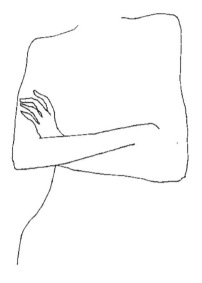

Don't take yourself out of this world, because of the
evil people you've crossed. You'll only be leaving
room for more bad people. You're good and your
story is meant to help somebody else, to remind
someone outside of you, that there's still good in this
world of occasional misfortune.

Hey, Lost child by Hogoe Elimiera

Is it a situation or a problem. A situation you can't change, it holds its own power of direction to work itself out. A problem you can change, it gives you the ability to create a solution to receive the answer you need.

Hey, Lost child by Hogoe Elimiera

Losing someone

1-2

1.

Within this room of diamonds and pearls I've built a
hill in the upstairs bedroom, no sound is to be made,
no room for a move to make. No space, because I've
made a bed out of the soil that I use as intake. The
pressure my casket consumes has buried me alive,
my heart speaks out to you, smiling faces and happy
lives.

2.

like a movie review never gone bad, my heart is
black as these walls glamoured with the dust of the
diamonds, whether diamonds or family tears I
couldn't tell for I was told there was no escape from
hell. May it be or wether I've yet to find the door,
darling listen here, don't bury your living soul in the
ground meant for the dead.

How sad you must be, to say goodbye to someone
you only remember saying hello to. How harsh it
must be to have lost a love you've grown accustom to
responding to. In the end one thing remains. You
can't die alive, to live with the dead. Time passes,
and sadness heals. It makes the happiness of moving
on that much sweeter.

Moving on never meant forget. Simply means
remembering to love yourself in the midst of
destruction and protecting yourself because no one
else will do it for you, as you deserve, but you.

At the age of eleven, I asked God why he took good people. An old man beside me responded in simplicity. " He clearly doesn't take all the good people, because you're still here to show someone else what Good can be."

When I was fourteen I asked a teacher: Does everything truthfully happen for a reason or is it the only answer that cancels out any guilt of inaccuracy. She has yet to write up an equation to answer the question I gave her, as easily as I did when I found " x" for her math test.

Who should you love, the one that loves you or the one you love. If you love yourself enough, you wouldn't be relying on the one that loves you, in fear of not being loved. You wouldn't be chasing that one that doesn't look your way, in heartache of not being enough. Someone will come along that admires the love you have for you, loving you as you should be loved, the way you should love you.

You've discredit your ability, due to your lack of stability. Are you wrong for your lack of structure in a game you have yet to understand. Truthfully it should be told the only stable thought that ever existed is the fact that nothing is ever stable.

Become consistent in the position that not everything
is consistent, remind someone that it's not a matter of
positive or negative because even in the negativity
there's positivity.

You can't concern the opinion of another on your work because it was your own work and diligence that created the masterpiece that now stands. For any opinion from another that is said, should lack your concern. But be thankful for it that they felt it was relevant enough to share words on something they hadn't created. It shows they care, even though, they they claim they never did.

love is consistently evolving too often to even place
in a dominant stage of endlessness. Why discredit
your days of growth towards self love, when what
you're trying to accomplish is about the change in
perspective not the speed in result.

Allow the past to make you better not bitter. Victory is never sweet on a sour tongue. Accomplishments are never seen with regretful eyes. Joy is never experienced with a lifeless heart. Experience is meant to educate not be a failure to your progress.

What is it that you can't believe is true exactly? I've been looking about and can't seem to find anything out of the ordinary that would give you such a surprise. You've always been this amazing, it's just that you're only now starting to realize.

You live in a world of "because i'm right. you must be wrong therefore I will not listen to you because you question my self made fact. " You're right to be confused, in a world where so many portray dominance, to everything. Yet, it's pretty obvious isn't it? It's a world of seeking souls, in search for guidance just as you do. Stubborn to admit fault, or correct perspective. You aren't the only one, you're just one of the ones that's admitted it so far. That's why you feel lonely.

Hey, Lost child by Hogoe Elimiera

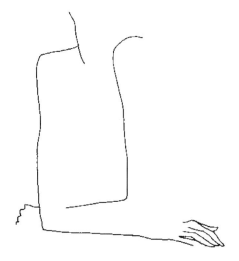

If you force a person into submission out of what you believe is just, you've contradicted your stand on what truly is just. Don't demand respect you were never going to receive. In the process you sell yourself short to someone that only ever saw you as clearance.

GM

The survivor shouldn't take responsibility for the
misfortune. The misfortune never intended for a
survivor, but you made it, so why are you
criminalizing yourself, over something you were a
victim to. Why are you feeling lost, when you clearly
won.

You are no less than the one you aspire to be. You have yet to accomplish the requirements your life steps listed for you in hope to achieve the results of your efforts. They will come, and when they do, you'll forget that you waited for your dreams to come true.

Hey, Lost child by Hogoe Elimiera

You've struggled to find the answer you need. Sometimes it's not the answer you want. Don't be discouraged yet, because you've only reached step three of a twelve questioned test.

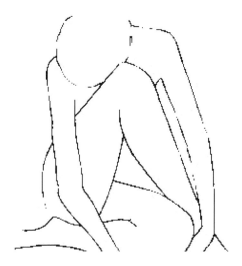

It's distasteful sometimes the efforts that are made, that don't match up with the results you're trying to create. Sometimes it's not the effort, you're just not yet really to carry the strength of the results.

Hey lost child,

You must've worried, you must've cried, you must've regretted the days that have gone by. How slowly they glided from place to place. You must've regretted the speed at which you established your methods. But relax you're doing fine. When In a maze the faster you try to get out without a plan, the further you get stuck within.

Hey, Lost child by Hogoe Elimiera

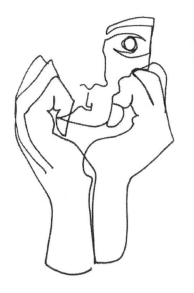

"JOANNE" Linework by Julia Hariri

Hey, Lost child by Hogoe Elimiera

You're a worthy being to a steadfast world. You are worthy because to the distinction that arose in your hinderance, you're still relevant. You're a bloom. A rose's bloom needed in a room of thorns. Petals cut at times, sometimes they fall, but even wilted at times, the bloom will always be the most beautiful among, a valley of thorns.

Hey, Lost child by Hogoe Elimiera

Hey, Lost child by Hogoe Elimiera

Letter to you

If no one told you today, I hope you know you have a
power in you. You have a purpose. What you want
will be achieved you will accomplish it.

About the author,

I am a twenty-year-old college student. I moved to the states at the age of six, from Lomé, Togo. Do I know what I am doing? Frankly no, but that's the beauty in the life we are living what you are to do comes looking for you.

I model, here and there and hope to get in more editorial work in the future. I have been writing to cope with my words since I was a child. I like many others wish success for myself so that I may one day be in the position to bring success to others.

Thank you for diving into my mind, and all the things I wish I could say, I hope it connected with you as they do with me.

Stay blessed beloved.

Hey, Lost child by Hogoe Elimiera

Ig: Negraitta.

Made in the USA
Columbia, SC
20 June 2020